The Squirrels' Thanksgiving

by Steven Kroll • illustrated by Jeni Bassett

SCHOLASTIC INC.
New York Toronto London Auckland Sydney

For Josephine and Richard Aldridge,
more than a special family

ISBN 0-590-10837-9

Text copyright © 1991 by Steven Kroll.
Illustrations copyright © 1991 by Jeni Bassett.
All rights reserved. Published by Scholastic Inc., 555 Broadway, New York, NY 10012, by arrangement with Holiday House, Inc.

12 11 10 9 8 7 6 5 4   0 1 2/0

Printed in the U.S.A.   24
First Scholastic printing, October 1997

The night before Thanksgiving, Momma and Poppa Squirrel and their two children, Brenda and Buddy, were relaxing in front of the fire.

"You know," Momma said, "Thanksgiving is such a lovely holiday. We have so much to be thankful for."

Poppa was rocking in his rocking chair. "It's true," he said. "We have our friends and our home, and of course we have our family."

Buddy and Brenda stopped shelling nuts. Brenda glared at Buddy. That afternoon, when they'd been counting acorns for Thanksgiving, Buddy had knocked Brenda's off the table.

He had also gotten glue on Brenda's fur
while they were making Pilgrim place mats
for the table.

Brenda wasn't thankful for Buddy at all.

Buddy glared at Brenda.

Earlier that day, they'd been gathering nuts for Momma's nut bread. Brenda had lagged behind and dropped her nuts all over the ground.

She had also put big marshmallows on the sweet potatoes when he had wanted little ones.

Buddy wasn't thankful for Brenda at all.

"Well, children," said Poppa, "it's time for bed. I hope that tomorrow you will show how thankful you are for one another."

"And," said Momma, "you should be thankful for your Aunt Nellie and Uncle Herb and your cousins, Penny and Chuck. They're coming for Thanksgiving dinner."

That night, Brenda tossed and turned, wondering how she could show she was thankful for her brother and for relatives she didn't know. Buddy, of course, wondered the same thing.

The next morning, Buddy and Brenda
bumped into each other in front of the bathroom.

"Please," said Buddy, opening the door,
"you first."

Brenda couldn't believe what she'd heard.
Buddy always ran into the bathroom before
she did. She spent an extra long time brush-
ing her teeth.

Then she went down to breakfast and poured Buddy a bowl of cereal.

"Thank you," said Buddy.

When the family went out to the car to go to church, Brenda jumped into the place Buddy had been promised in the front seat.

Buddy was about to say something mean. Then he remembered it was Thanksgiving. "I hope you'll enjoy your ride," he said to Brenda, and slunk into the back.

Buddy and Brenda were behaving so po-
litely that Momma and Poppa Squirrel were
smiling happily when they reached the
church. They all marched up the aisle to a
front pew and waited for the service to begin.

They had to wait a long time. Buddy and
Brenda began to get restless.

Buddy leaned over and started making gargling noises at Brenda. Brenda made gargling
noises back.

"Shhhhh!" cried Momma Squirrel. "Both
of you, stop it!"

Buddy and Brenda settled down, but the service still didn't begin. Buddy leaned over and pinched Brenda on the leg. "Owwwww!" she said. She pinched Buddy back.

"Ouch!" he screeched.
"All right," said Poppa Squirrel. "Enough's enough. Remember what Momma and I told you about being thankful."

When the service began, Buddy and
Brenda tried to remember the good things
about each other. They were quiet, and they
behaved.

After church, they all piled into the car and drove home. Aunt Nellie and Uncle Herb and the cousins, Penny and Chuck, were waiting at the hollow tree.

"Happy Thanksgiving," said Poppa Squirrel.

"We're so glad to see you," said Momma
Squirrel.

Brenda and Buddy smiled at their cousins.
"Do you want to come see our toys?" they
asked.

Penny and Chuck didn't answer. Instead, Penny stepped hard on Buddy's toe.

Chuck gave Brenda an elbow in the ribs.

"Ow!" said Buddy.
"Cut it out!" said Brenda.

Poppa and Momma glared. Buddy and
Brenda looked at one another. How could
they be thankful for their cousins? They were
mean.

"Well," said Momma Squirrel, "it's time to
eat now. Let's all go inside."

A big bowl of nuts and acorns was in front of each place. There were serving dishes filled with cranberries and squash and sweet potatoes topped with big marshmallows. In the middle was the loaf of golden brown nut bread Momma Squirrel had baked that morning.

"Let's join hands before we begin," said Poppa Squirrel.

Penny put her hands behind her back. "I won't hold hands with Chuck," she said.

"I won't hold hands with Penny either," said Chuck.

Brenda grabbed Chuck's hand. Buddy grabbed Penny's hand. Poppa said grace, and the meal began.

Buddy dug into a thick slice of nut bread.
He began eating his squash. Suddenly Penny
dumped a pawful of nuts down his back!

"Hey," said Buddy, "stop it!"

"Now, Penny," said Uncle Herb, "that is
not the way to enjoy Thanksgiving dinner.
You might prefer eating it instead."

Penny paid no attention. She turned and dumped some acorns down Chuck's back.

Chuck pulled her tail.

Then he pulled Brenda's tail, too.

"Ow!" said Brenda. "That hurt!"

Chuck jumped up and knocked over a pitcher of cider.

"This has gone far enough!" said Poppa, mopping cider out of his lap.

"Yuk!" said Brenda. "Our cousins are really awful!"

"They're much worse than we've ever been," said Buddy.

"I think we'd better leave," said Aunt Nellie. "We'll come back when our children can behave. We'll call you later."

After they had all left, Momma and Poppa Squirrel sat down once more with Buddy and Brenda.

"What a relief!" said Momma.

"Now we can enjoy our Thanksgiving in peace," said Poppa.

"At least I hope we can," said Momma, looking at Brenda and Buddy.

"I guess I do have a lot to be thankful for," said Brenda. "Buddy's really not so bad."

"At least we can do things together," said Buddy. "We can shell nuts and count acorns and make place mats."

"Let's have another blessing," said Poppa Squirrel.

They took each other's hands.

"Thanks for this good food and our good family," said
Poppa.

"Thanks for Buddy," said Brenda.

"Thanks for Brenda," said Buddy.

And they all ate their delicious Thanksgiving dinner.